Tuppence

Tuppence has lost something very special.

She needs **HELP !!!!!**

This is the tail of Tuppence who lives in "The Yard".

She has a white whisker
and an ear that is scarred.

With beautiful eyes, one yellow, one green.

Her red collar has diamonds, befitting a queen.

Her fur is dark grey and as soft as can be.

Which she cleans ......

..........and she preens, no home for a flea.

Her most treasured possession is a deep trilling …

PURRRRR.

That becomes quite deafening when stroking her fur.

But although Tuppence looked cute and purrrrfectly pretty.

She was actually a mean, bad tempered grey kitty.

HISS
HISS
HISS

She loved chasing the chickens,

...... making the ducks cry quack, quack.

Shouting "Out of my way, you're under ... **ATTACK !**"

Then with great speed, up a tree she would climb.

Scaring the chicks ...sneering, "It's breakfast time !!"

Another favourite game was to hide,
down by the river.

Where she'd frighten the fish, making them shiver and quiver.

But one terrible morning, Tuppence woke up and found......

As she tried to **PURRR** .... there wasn't a sound.

She tried …….

and she tried …

but only a fur ball appeared.

"Oh no " she howled, "This is worse than I feared".

"What can I do ?" she sobbed to a spider named Fred.

Who whispered "See Bert", then ran up his thread.

"Why yes"… she meowed, "Bert will help me I'm sure".
"With magical potions, there must be a cure !!"

So scampering off, towards the sound of a flute.

Finding Bert in the sun, in a very pink suit.

"Greetings Tuppence" he called,
"Do tell me what's wrong".

So she told him her story,
as he put his clothes on.

Bert listened closely, then when she'd finished he sighed.

"Tuppence you need to be more ....

JEKYLL ...

than .....**HYDE**".

If you stop all the fighting,
    make friends and just play.

Your purr might return to you,
    one sunny day.

Tuppence thought for a moment, then groaned "Yes you're right".
"I enjoy being mean and having a fight".

"My purr was special and I'm so sad it's gone".
"I know in my heart, that being a bully is wrong".

So she sat there and puzzled ……
would it be all that hard….

Tiggy

Ladybug

Tickle

Rabby

Rats

To be friendly and kind,

to all in "The Yard".

Tumbleweed

chickens

Chicks

To get her purr back,

she'd do what was required.

But all this running around,

was making her tired.

"Bert " she yawned ... "From today you will see".
"That I am true to my word ....

a quite different me".

So she stopped chasing and hissing, wasn't naughty or rude.
Even offering the rats, her left over food.

Playing with the chicks, as she lay in the sun.
They fluttered and giggled and had lots of fun.

Then down by the river, she didn't frighten the fish.
Just dreamt they were served, piled high on a dish.

As the days passed,
   she became more thoughtful and kind.

"Bert I'm so happy I left....
      my mean ways behind".

"I do miss my purr, but have lots of friends now".

"Your advice was just right"…...he gave a small bow.

In fact all in "The Yard" were really impressed.

So a surprise party was planned, Tuppence being star guest.

"Oh how wonderful" she declared, as they brought out the cake.
With one candle on top, a wish she would make.

Then suddenly without warning, she felt a warm fuzzy glow.
A small sound could be heard and it started to grow.

It became louder and louder……. why, it was purrrfectly clear.
Her purr had returned….

PURR

PURR

PURR

PURR

everyone gave a big ....

Tumbleweed has only one leg, which makes life very difficult on the farm. What makes it worse is that the naughty wind tries to blow him over all the time….

Can his new friend Bert help!!!

All Tumbleweed wants, is to be like his friends and play.

Can Bert really make this happen!!!!

ISBN 978-0-9562831-0-8

Tiggy is not very happy. She does not like the way she looks. Maybe if she had long legs, or a different nose or even fur ……

She asks her friend Bert to help, but things do not go quite as planned!!!!!

ISBN 978-0-9562831-1-5

Tickle loves to play with his friend…..and flying a kite sounds like great fun…….unfortunately it is not easy for a small hedgehog.

To make things worse Tickle forgets to tell his mum, and she gets very worried when she can't find him

Can Bert save the day again!!!

ISBN 978-0-9562831– 2-2